RETURN TO PINE STREET:

RENEE WALKER'S HAUNTING

By Cassie Williams

booksbycassie.com

Nothing on this earth is ever lost; it may change shape, color, and density, it may move to another place... though it still remains.

Albert Einstein

2013

All rights reserved. No part of this publication can be reproduced, stored in a retrieval system, or transmitted in any form or by any means, electronic, mechanical, photocopying, recording or otherwise, without the prior permission of the publishers and/or author.

Kindle: ASIN: B00FJGO8NU

Paperback: ISBN-10: 1492864366

ISBN-13: 978-1492864363

Table of Contents

1 1
2 5
3 10
4 12
5 19
6 24
7 27
8 31
9 35
10 40
11 49
12 53
13 55
14 56
15 61
16 65
17 66
18 69
19 71
20 73
21 78
22 82
23 84
24 88
25 90

26	92
27	97
28	103
29	104
30	107
31	110
32	112
33	115
34	117
35	125
36	127
37	135
38	136

1

Renee Walker opened her eyes, panting heavily. This was her usual wake up call. Streams of light beat on her face through the blinds, pulling her back into reality. The dreadful realization that this was the start of another day, to repeat the previous day, to relive the previous night and the ones before that, made her pray for an end to it all. At the same time, through her helpless cries, she's glad still that it's morning and longed to move to the farthest points north where there might be six months of rest. However wrong that may be, she still felt somewhat safer in the daylight...somewhat.

"Devin, Andrew, Nicole, it's time to get up!" Renee yelled as she passed the kids' bedrooms, putting on her shoe as she headed toward the kitchen, pausing only to flip the bathroom light off. "Come on guys. It's Monday, work and school."

Nicole came into the kitchen squinting her eyes, rubbing them as she tries to convince her mother, again, that she's too sick to go today.

"Go get dressed and come get some breakfast and you'll feel better." she said as Nicole stomped to her room, her long, dark hair flowing mad in the breeze.

Mornings are usually pretty frantic and rushed at the Walker house. Like the aftermath of a storm that hit during the night, people trying to pick up the pieces and put them together again, frayed as they may be. Luckily each one still fits, somehow. For now anyway.

Devin stood in the doorway watching his mother pack their lunches as though nothing happened. "You need to rest." he said.

Renee glanced at her oldest son's worried face; the one who's seen the most, too much in his fourteen years. She hated to see the way he looked at her. His big brown eyes, soft and caring, peered through her, searching for more than words. She wanted to be stronger for him, for all of them. She wanted them to have the normal childhood she never had. Her mother, sad and reclusive after Renee's father died when she was a toddler, stayed mostly to herself. She remarried, briefly, unhappily, for financial reasons after becoming pregnant again when Renee was eleven. The divorce left her even more strapped which forced them to move into an old, worn down house. The house that started it all, the snowball effect into Renee's life now. She tries desperately to keep her children sheltered from herself. To keep them occupied, involved in their time, safe. What she thought a mother should be. She wanted to say that it's over, things will be alright. She knew it would be a lie. She grinned and, knowing he's getting too old to be fooled, said "I will."

Devin watched his mother's face in the rearview mirror. He studied the spheres under her eyes and the deep lines at the corners of them. He remembered them being there when he was little, faintly, not like they were now. She was once so full of life and energy. He was proud of how beautiful she was; admired her tan complexion, long black hair and smooth skin. Something has stolen her youthfulness from him though. Her skin looks pale and tired, reminding him of the old lady telling a story from her deathbed at the start of a movie. Her graying hair lies limply in a bun, as lifeless as her face appears. He knew she shouldn't look like this at thirty-five, not like this at all.

"Bye boys, love you!" Renee said as they got out of the car.

"Love ya ma." Andrew said jogging away.

Devin looked into his mother's eyes, "Love you too mom." The car drove away, leaving him watching to ensure that she was safe before heading to the building.

"Now let's catch that bus." Renee said, smiling at Nicole.

2

Renee pulled into the parking lot at work. Staring at the entrance, she wondered how she would get through another day when all she wanted to do was go to sleep right there in the car. Sleep with the sun shining on her skin, warming her, protecting her. For that, she would give almost anything. She sleeps in shifts, mostly during daylight hours – as dawn approaches, after work, sometimes just before dusk. Whenever she can and sometimes when she can't help it. Summer months bring the most rest but those are short lived. This is the time of year she hates; the Midwest, early falls…early darkness. She looked at her watch, disgusted by the glimpse she caught of herself, flipped the mirror over and got out.

"Good morning." Sharon said.

"I hope so."

Renee sat at her desk next to Sharon's. There wasn't much room for both of them in the little office. Maybe that's what made them become so close. Maybe it's the way Sharon looked out for her, worrying about her sleep, constantly cheering her up; things her mother never did. At least not since she moved out when she was a teenager, after that horrible night. The night Renee wished she could remember, redo, forget. Sharon is the closest thing she's had to a mother for some time, even still, that night is something she's never spoken of.

"You're going to do it, aren't you?" Sharon asked.

Renee shrugged her shoulders, "I guess it can't hurt."

"Good, something has to help you sleep. Girl you look like crap!" she chuckled as she answered the phone.

Renee went to work, easily distracted by the hustle of people going by the door. Selma and George wheeled by, stopped to wave. They're planning to get married next spring, proof that life continues when you live in a nursing home. They brought spirit to the building and the workers loved to hear their stories of lives well lived. Optimistic even through the hard times, of which they've had their fair share.

After lunch, Ruth came in for her daily visit. She's Renee's favorite. Such a tiny woman, her white hair flowing out from under the helmet she has to wear. "Na now now now." She mumbled as she leaned forward in her wheelchair, grabbing at something only she sees on the floor.

Renee knelt in front of her to scoot her back. "Hi there Ruthie." she said bobbing her head from side to side in front of her, trying to get some kind of eye contact. Ruth stares at her mouth as if she's trying to figure out what she's saying but her eyes look so far away. She starts to snatch the papers on Sharon's desk.

"Na now now na dut dut dut."

"See ya later Ruth." Sharon waved as Renee wheeled her out of the office. "Another crash, head first, diverted!"

Renee sat back at her desk, running her hands across her face. Although promising she would, she didn't know if she could go through with it. The thought of it alone terrified her. *The kids can't keep seeing me like this,* she thought as she held her forehead up with her hands, trying to stay awake. She's been seeing a therapist, at Sharon's suggestion and her husband's approval, once a week for the last month. The doctor knows how poorly she sleeps, the nightmares she wakes from, the sleep walking, and the engrossing fear of the dark. Renee told her it began when she was younger only worsening through the years. The doctor, new to her practice and out to save the world, assured Renee she could help her if she was willing to face her fears head on.

She missed her mother terribly. Aside from jeopardizing her own children, she'd risk anything to find out what happened that night. To see her mother again, to be held and loved by her again. She felt like a little girl, not her age at all. *I'm not a child anymore. I'm grown for God's sake!* She struggled for sanity when she heard children laughing. A little girl holding her mother's hand as they walk down the sidewalk fills her with jealously. Even holding her own daughters hand makes her feel guilty at the time she's lost with her mother. Resentment, spiteful at times. She knows it's wrong, she knows it sounds crazy, yet she can't help it.

A collage of memories, like photos pinned to a bulletin board, she never feels like she's really there. Gliding through life, unlived. She's a shell. *If they only knew.* She thought, of her deepest thoughts, if they only knew she was an empty shell, breathing and eating and faking all the way through. She wanted more than anything to be the perfect mother. To be there in the moment, to protect them from the things in this world she could see and couldn't. *They must never know.*

Desperate, she agreed to let the doctor do her will. Reluctantly agreeing to let her dive into the darkest parts of her head, let her open the gates that have been locked and double locked and buried as far down as they would go. *She'll think I'm crazy. She'll have my kids taken from me.* Maybe that would be best, and maybe it would be.

"It's time, I better go." Renee said.

3

Littletin is a town reminiscent of a small farm community just outside Alton, Illinois. Only a few miles long, most of its population are descendants well known to one another, trapped together in the grips of small town life. A few drifters have settled there, mostly workers who got caught in the small towns trap after the expansion of the oil pipeline a few years ago. The rest are reformed city dwellers, tired of the hustle and bustle, looking for the slower life.

The main part of town was built more recently, within the last fifty years. It looks like any other city with similar houses built too close together, small yards and a business section down the main road appropriately named Main St. The old part of town lies in the outskirts. There are many houses left that were built in the late 1800's to early 1900's. Those, too, all resemble one another. Farm houses without the farm, turned rental property for those who couldn't afford to live in the neighborhoods.

The oldest house sits on the edge of the town's limits; unrentable these days. The houses leading to it become fewer, with more open fields in between. The dead end road is filled with potholes just past Old Man Willie's house. The long rock driveway gives visitors plenty of time to turn after seeing its condition. One dying bare tree sits in front. An open field of weeds and dead wheat grains sits at the side of the house for as far as the eye can see. Nothing grows in the soil, nothing survives. The house is small, probably meant to hold only one, maybe two. It has a basement with a concrete floor and crumbling stone walls. The low ceiling has spider webs hanging off the pipes and water dripping down into puddles. There's a small room just at the end of the steps and another a few feet past that at the back of the basement. They were used for storage for most previous inhabitants.

4

The brief drive didn't leave time for Renee to think about what she was doing. One of the perks, and downfalls, to living in a small town. The tall, five-story glass building seemed so out of place. Renee thought it looked akin to something that belonged in a big city. Not here, where the buildings are brick, old stone. Dusty brown and run down looking, like the people in them. She was nervous, fidgeting in her seat.

Renee hasn't told the doctor much more than of her nightmares. Afraid of revealing too much. All she needed was to sleep, unafraid, through the nights. That's all she needed the doctor to do. Anything more would be unnecessary. Silly, even she knows it's silly if you say it out loud. It was crazy, so she kept it to herself, not telling even her husband. The man who saved her from being homeless, taking her in without question. The man who protected her and cared for her and loved her through all of these years; believing in everything she says and does. The man she adored for all of these things didn't earn enough of her trust to be told the truth. *They'll have me locked away,* she thought if she told anyone. *Nightmares, that's all they are.*

It was time to go in. She didn't move. *I promised I would try it.* Though she didn't believe it would help, or even work, she did promise and that was something she would not break.

"Nice to see you again." Dr. Dagen said.

Renee surveyed the room. The walls had an almost unnoticeable yellow hue with a white, puffy leather couch and chair in the middle of the room. The furniture: desk, end tables, coffee table and bookshelves were slick black. It all looked sophisticated. All expect the curtains. They were a heavy, frumpy material all bundled up in a mess from floor to ceiling, opened up at either side of the window.

"Let's get started. Lay on the couch." she ordered as she drew them, barely able to get them closed.

Renee stood as the last ray of sunlight disappeared as the doctor sealed the two ends together. The rush of a cold, clammy sweat started to form in the palms of her hands. Her mouth started to water, she gulped down, unsure if the doctor could see her trembles in the dark. *Where's a light?* She panicked. The doctor had no idea how afraid of the dark she was. Not the still dark, that's just the waiting period, but when the darkness moves. When she realized for the first time that there are different shades of black, unrecognizable until part of it shifts away from the rest slowly, quietly, purposefully. That's when she knew that things weren't what they seem. Nothing ever is. She wanted to run out of the room. Her body wouldn't budge. Terrified by the thought of letting someone in - of letting secrets out, she still stood.

Renee pulled away when the doctor touched her hand; certain she felt the trembling. The doctor guided her with a nudge on her shoulder to the couch. "I'm going to put you under so that it will be easier to recall some things that you may not be aware of." The doctor continued, "We will find the key to release you from it."

Renee started to object. The doctor tilted her head up a little as she kept talking, taking full control as she laid her down.

"I'm going to swing this light back and forth over you and count backwards. We'll start off slow."

The room appeared to close in as the little stream of light swung back and forth from the pen. Dr. Dagen looked so much older in that light. Her pasty colored skin looked tarnished now; her glasses seemed to engulf her face.

"Just relax and breathe deeply. Watch the light and let your mind go back to when you were younger, when you were five. I'm going to count from ten and when I get to one, you will be under. You will be able to hear me and talk to me. When I say stop you will wake up and remember everything."

Her voice, soft and soothing, almost whispering. Her lips were moving normally though the words seemed to drag out, not coinciding with her mouth. The ticking of the clock echoed in her head. "Ten (tick), nine (tick), eight (tick)…"

That's all Renee heard of the counting. She opened her eyes not believing that it worked.

"Where are you?" the doctor asked.

Renee looked around the familiar house. She sat on the floor in front of a small box of toys. She held a Barbie doll in her hand. "I'm at my Grandma's house." she said in a small child's voice.

"Who's with you?"

The house was still. The clock on the wall ticked slower. "I'm alone." she said as she slipped a pair of pants on the doll.

"You're only five Renee, someone has to be there."

Someone has to be there. Renee remembered sitting alone, day after day, playing with her dolls. *Just a shell.* "My mom is in her room. She's always locked in her room."

"Well go see her."

Renee looked at the door of the quiet room. Nothing but the incessant ticking stirred. "I don't go in there." she said as her small hands dug through the box.

The doctor wrote in her notebook, sure that Renee's problems lie in her childhood, somewhere with her mother. "Okay, close your eyes. We'll try again."

Renee put the toys down and covered her face with her hands.

"Open your eyes Renee. You're seven now, what do you see?" the doctor asked.

She pulled her hands down. "I'm in my bedroom."

"And where is that?"

"One of the houses we lived in. We moved a lot."

"Is anyone there?"

Renee sat on her bed. *Tick, tick, tick...* "I'm alone."

"Stop." The doctor put her pen and notebook down, frustrated. She opened the curtains. "I think you're blocking me Renee." she said walking back to the chair.

Renee squinted from the rush of light. "I'm sorry, I didn't mean to."

"Were there any memories with your family?"

Saddened by her question, Renee tried to remember. "I was alone a lot, except when I saw my Grandma."

"Alright, we'll stop for today but I want you to be ready next time. Really concentrate."

Renee left. The doctor sat at her desk. "She's repressing." she said into her recorder. "I'll need to get more aggressive next time." She continued writing on her notepad.

5

It's nine o'clock Thursday evening, one day before Andrew's big basketball game at the Rec Center and it's all he could talk about for weeks. Devin's helping him practice in the backyard and Nicole is cheering them on. She feels guilty and switches sides, no playing favorites.

Renee made a few phone calls to put the last pieces in place for the surprise party after the game.

"Is everything ready?" Mike whispered.

"Looks like it, hope I didn't miss anything." Renee said, hanging up the phone.

"You rented the fitness center, ordered the cake and invited everyone. What else is there?"

Renee gave him a look that let him know it wasn't as easy as that. "I wish you could go to at least one practice before the season is over." She tried to sound more like he was missing out instead of complaining that he put work before his family.

"Me too, but you know I have a late meeting every Thursday." Adding defensively, "You don't always make it either. We have jobs you know."

"It's better than none." *And I'm always there to pick him up.* She thought, not daring to say it out loud, not after tonight.

It was ten after six, fifteen minutes late. She was tired and forgot about practice and went straight home after picking Nicole up from the sitter's. She saw Andrew sitting on the bench, waiting. It's the middle of fall so dusk comes by four-thirty already. Only a couple cars were left in front yet the lights were still on. He gave her a scowl. Disappointment. He opened the door to the backseat and plopped down.

"You're late." his voice shaky.

He may be tall but still only twelve years old. Uncertain if he was upset with her for being late or for allowing himself to get scared, Renee thought better not to push it. "Sorry, I lost track of time."

It was quiet the rest of the way home. The only sound was from the dried up leaves blowing around in the wind. Renee promised herself she wouldn't be late again. The silent treatment he gave was deafening, but the look on his face as he stared out the window and tried to stop his bottom lip from uncontrollably making a frown broke her heart.

"I just wish they would have it on a different day." Mike said, interrupting her thoughts.

Nicole ran into the house, "I have to get this outfit off!" she hollered.

"Stop running!" Mike and Renee shouted at the same time.

Nicole wanted to be a cheerleader for Andrew's team since she was five but this is the first year she's been old enough. After watching and practicing for six years, she was a shoo-in to make the team.

Devin is a different story. He likes to play sports when he wants, not on a schedule. Usually what he wants to do is play video games. He's even talked about going to college to become a programmer. No doubt in Renee's mind that he would be good at it with all his experience playing them.

"It's time for bed." Renee said as the boys came in. "School tomorrow and you have a busy day Andrew."

"I know, love you mom." he bent down to kiss her cheek. "Goodnight."

"Night mom." Devin said as he went to his room.

"Love ya." she yelled as he closed his door.

Renee went into Nicole's room and tucked her in with the covers under her body so that nothing could get in. Nicole holds the top of them up to her neck. *Just like me,* she thought.

Renee sat in the recliner, her head bobbing as the words ran together in the book that was to keep her awake. Her head jerked. The house was still. The light from the lamp barely reached the middle of the room. Mike was asleep already. It was time. She made sure the kids were asleep before turning on the bathroom light and heading to her room.

Mike woke as she climbed in bed, careful not to let her know. He dozed in and out through the night listening to the whispering, "eighteen, nineteen, twenty…" The whispering he heard night after night; the tossing and turning, the up and down. He learned to sleep through it but still wakes when she gets in or out of bed, always looking at the time on the clock. In the beginning, he'd wished he could help her, hold her, calm her. Now he only wishes for morning so she can let herself fall asleep for an hour before the alarm goes off.

6

Melissa Dagen just finished emptying more boxes in the master bedroom of her Victorian-style house. She and her husband, Tom, bought it this past summer, preparing to move back home so she could open her own practice after finishing school. They had some money left from the trust fund she received when she turned eighteen but her education in Chicago and the houses in Alton were expensive, which is where her heart was set on settling down. The strain of the dwindling fund led her to look into a practice nearby in Littletin. It's not where she wants her career to take off but she knows she has to start somewhere and the price was right for now.

She's a young doctor, in her early thirties, who married her high school boyfriend. Privileged from the beginning, she was unsure if the people of Littletin were the kind of people she would feel comfortable with. A snoot is what they called her, just as she generalized all of them as hicks. It was only a few minutes outside of Alton though, so she decided to do most of her marketing there and hoped that people would make the short drive to see her. She wants to work with troubled teens; she thought her compassion and strong family upbringing put her at a good advantage to really help them.

"I'm beat!" Tom said as he carried another box from the lower level into the room.

She kissed the side of his lips, rubbed her hands down the muscles bulging on his biceps as he sat the box on the floor in front of their bed "I think we're done for today, there's always tomorrow to look forward to." she said. "Just as long as it's done in time for the party on Saturday."

He turned, pulling her into him, sweat rolling down his temple, "Well if you rub me like that again we'll have to start on tonight."

She giggled, kissed him again and ran to the bed and jumped on it, lifting her once white tank top over her head. "I love the nights." she teased.

Tom pounced on the bed, crawling over to her, "Well, well Dr. Dagen. Let's see if I can give you something to talk into your little recorder about." He kissed her, pushing her onto the pillow as he twisted the switch on the lamp.

7

"Oh I remember your grandmother so well. Such a dear woman." Selma said.

"Yes, she is." Renee smiled, remembering how much she loved her Grandma.

"Invite her to the wedding for us." George said as he put his hand on top of Selma's.

"I will do that." Renee said, excusing herself to answer her phone.

"Mrs. Walker?" the man asked.

"Yes, this is her."

"This is Principal Smith. We need you to come to the school. Your son, Devin, has been in a fight."

"I have to go." she told Sharon as she left the office, stopping to turn Ruth's chair away from the entrance.

She went into the principal's office. He stood behind the counter; tall, business-like, authoritative. "Both boys will be suspended Monday. No matter who started it. I'm sorry but it's school policy." he said.

Devin got in the car. He had a red mark on the side of his nose.

"What happened?" she asked, checking his face.

He jerked away. "Nothing."

"I know you Devin. You didn't fight for no reason. That's not like you." she said.

He looked over at her with tears in his eyes. "I don't want to talk about it."

She lifted his chin, "Tell me."

"He was making fun of you, okay?!" he yelled.

Renee remembered how kids would make fun of her for being quiet. It started in elementary and continued through high school. It hurt but she never said anything back. "Well I don't care what people think of me and you shouldn't let them bother you either."

"They always say things. Their parents won't let them come over because you're weird. I don't like it!" he slammed his hands on his legs.

Renee gave him a minute to cry. *He's defending you, just like Mike had to.*

She was sixteen when they met, working at a café to feed herself. Mike was new in town, coming here to put in a new pipeline for the refinery a few towns away. She was stricken by his hard, manly features. He came to the café every day and sat at her table. She felt safe with him. He was drawn to her. After finding out she was on her own he moved her into his house and asked her to marry him despite what the town said. She felt loved and wanted, wasting no time saying yes.

This town, she thought, *busybodies!*

"You can't control other people Devin, only yourself. Hitting someone won't change what they think." she said as she hugged him, wiping tears off his face.

8

"Go Panthers!" Renee chanted as the team came darting into the gym.

"Alright Renee, sit down." Mike said embarrassed.

Renee can't help feeling the adrenaline watching her son running, dribbling the ball so fast that no one can catch him. She's alive, for the first time in years, she's alive! Like she's running with him, watching over her shoulder to make sure there isn't a thief about to steal the ball. The time flies when they're playing, especially when they're winning. It's twenty-nine to twenty-eight in the last quarter. The other team has the ball, Jake McAllister. Jake from the Wood River Vikings. He is the one who can run side by side down the court with Andrew. He is the one who last year, and on purpose in Renee's eyes, tripped Andrew and stole the ball to make the winning shot. *Crooked Refs!* They didn't even call a foul; they said they didn't see it.

It's Andrew's chance now. Renee saw the look on his face as Jake ran toward him. *Redemption.* She feels it too. *Get the ball and keep him from making the winning shot.* She looked at the clock…twenty-five seconds left; time seems to slow in Jake's favor. He's almost to the basket when Andrew ran so fast that he was right behind him.

She jumped to her feet, yelling as loud as her small voice would allow, "Get the ball!" With Mike and Devin on either side of her, drowning out her chants with their screams.

The auditorium exploded when Andrew reached his hand down just as he passed by Jake and when he turned the moment Jake jumped up to make a shot; he had brought the ball with him. The buzzer buzzed, the crowd cheered and the team held Andrew high up in the air.

"Great game!" One of the team fathers said on the way to the car.

"You know it was." Mike boasted with his chest pumped out.

They piled in the car. The kids were too busy bouncing around, rehashing the game to notice which direction they were going. Mike and Renee exchanged smirks as they listened to the laughter in the backseat.

"Why are we here?" Nicole asked.

"Just go inside."

The kids flung the doors open and ran inside as they saw the team cars pulling in.

"It's perfect." Mike said. Balloons floated up to the ceiling and covered the floor. Ribbons of purple and blue hung down. Drinks and a cake decorated the table off to the side.

"Cool!"

"Awesome!"

"Come on."

Kids screeched from all directions. The girls started a cheer on the bouncing floor, boys jumped off the trampolines into the ball pits. Parents gathered for seconds of the cake, talking about the game.

"Renee." She heard a whisper in her ear. She turned, her hair gently sliding up from the air.

"I'm ready for bed." Mike said as he came up behind her.

Renee sighed, "You scared me to death."

The kids fell asleep on the ride home. Renee tucked them in, something the boys haven't allowed for some time. Mike closed the bathroom door a little to create a vague glow in the bedroom. The adrenaline was gone. Mike ran his fingers across the hallows under Renee's eyes, preparing for the night. He kissed her on top of the head before rolling over, knowing she would lie awake until morning.

9

"Is everyone ready?" Renee called out heading toward the door. "We'll be late for the sermon."

The one thing she hated to be late for was church. Do gooder's snicker, calling them "those" people. *"Those horrible people"*. Mike knows, he helps her get them moving on Sunday morning so he doesn't have to listen to her preach all the way there.

The sun's shining, Indian summer, *magnificent.* Pastor Dave stood on the steps, shaking hands as people went inside. He's a tall, slender man. His graying blonde hair, greased back, revealed his red undertone face. He continually looked like he just finished shouting about something that he's so passionate about that his blood's boiling. His wife stood beside him, a mousy woman who gets lost in his presence.

"How nice to see you again Mike." Pastor Dave said, stretching out his welcoming hand.

"Wouldn't miss it for the world." Mike said.

Renee searched for her Grandma and Aunt Gladys. She wasn't really her aunt but everyone in town calls her that. She spotted them in the front. Her Grandma's short plump frame was heightened by the bun she wears her long black hair in and smushes it up in the air. A sweet woman who constantly has a hug and kiss on the cheek for anyone she sees, smiling the whole time. "Precious." She says as she leans in to plant one on your face. Gladys is just as kind, toting the same hair, with an Olive Oil-esque shape.

Pentecostal. Holy Rollers. That's what they call us. Renee thought as the church grew louder with praying and shouts of "Amen" and "Hallelujah" from all directions. The energy in the church is electrifying when Pastor Dave gets into it. Women jump up and bounce a little in place with their eyes closed, hands stretched up - reaching for the Messiah, smiling and crying at the same time. Right on cue, Gladys starts crying out in tongues. The church sits down to listen as another woman on the other side rises to her feet like a puppet and begins to translate the prayer. *Powerful. Exhilarating and calming.*

"Demons." Pastor Dave bellowed, capturing the attention in the room. "Today I want to talk about the demons in our lives."

The church grew noisy with fidgeting and sitting up straighter. She could almost read the looks on their faces. *Is he going to point out my demons?* Everyone has secrets. You just don't know who's talking about yours when you live in a small town.

"…If you smoke, you have a demon. If you drink, you have a demon. If you talk up one side and down your neighbors back side, you have a demon!" He pointed to one of the women. "Anything that keeps you from being you and right with God is your demon!" He hopped and hollered out as though he was reading Renee's mind. "You know, Sister Mary came to me the other day and told me that her Grandma over in St. Louis has been diagnosed with Alzheimer's and she asked me to pray for her."

Sister Mary nodded her permission.

"I'm asking this church, my church, our church to pray for her." His voice rising higher with each word. "But don't pray for her to be healed. No, no, no…she's already been healed. Jesus did that when he let them hammer him to the cross for her!"

The church erupted with exclamations of "Amen".

"I want you to pray to cast out her demons!" he commanded. "Pray that Jesus will take her demons that keep her from being her and right with God and cast them out as he did in Gadarenes and Capernaum."

Hands flew in the air, tears rolled to the ground, as the church prayed and begged for Jesus to cast out their demons. Pastor Dave came down in the pews and began praying for people individually with his hand on their foreheads while droplets of sweat rolled down his face from squinting his eyes so tight as he prayed.

"In Jesus name, cast out her demons and keep her right with God!" he shouted as each person fell back into their seats.

"That was scary." Mike whispered, walking out to the lobby, still not comfortable with such a change from being raised Catholic.

"Mom, look what I made!" Nicole said, running out of her youth group class holding a picture.

Renee knelt down and took the paper. She smiled up at Mike and saw his uneasiness, "Let's go guys."

10

"How have you been?" Dr. Dagen asked.

Renee sat on the couch. "Things have been going pretty good since last week." She straightened up, "That's actually what I wanted to talk to you about."

"Alright." Dr. Dagen leaned forward.

"I'm not sure what happened here last time, but it was good." she cleared her throat and squirmed on the seat. "I don't think I need to come anymore."

The doctor pushed her glasses up with her index finger, began to tap her chin with her pencil. "I'm not sure you've dealt with the real issues yet." she paused. "How's your mother?"

The room was silent.

"You're running. Stay with me and stop running. If you let me, I can help you." she pleaded. "What did you think about the hypnosis?"

Renee pushed aside the things that popped in her mind. Not wanting to reveal too much, to sound scared, to sound crazy, "It felt real," is all she managed to say.

"I'm sure it did." she chuckled. "Look Renee, your nightmares are just the tip of the iceberg here. I believe the real issues are with the way things ended with your family. You said you haven't seen them since you moved out of that house when you were fifteen." She looked down at her notes. "Fifteen is that right? "

Renee nodded.

"Alright, we need more time together. We need to deal with both things. I want to start seeing you on Thursday's too. I will not give up on you so don't you do it to me!" the doctor smiled.

Renee so wanted to see her mother again. *Could she really help me?* Renee wondered, could the doctor, confident and sure of herself, fix it all? Fix this shell? She didn't want to break her promise. She was exhausted. Her thoughts skipped erratically. She looked at her doctor, who seemed to care, to want to help. Renee agreed.

"Alright then, let's get started."

Renee rested her head on the pillow as the doctor closed the curtains.

"We need to try something else. I want to take you to the house."

Her eyes narrowed. "No," she sat up, "I don't want to go there."

"It's only a memory Renee and I'm here with you. I'll stop it if it gets to be too much, I promise." She grabbed her pen light.

Renee's breathing grew heavy. The dark room shifted, she knew it. She looked around as the steady stream made the rest of the room disappear into the deepest blackness. *Tick, tick, tick...*

"I promise." she said. "Ten, nine, eight, s-e-v-e-n…" The words slowed and slurred, until Renee opened her eyes.

She felt weak, sick to her stomach. She stood outside; a speck in the yard, looking up at the tiny house that seemed to be larger than anything she's seen. She was drawn to it. The house shrank in stature as she was pulled closer into it, not moving her body at all. There was no escape, she always knew it. The edges of the earth dropped at each squared corner of the parcel leaving only her and the house, the only things left in the world. Blackness surrounded them. Renee felt uncomfortable at how comfortable she was, like she was home after a lifetime of searching. The grass was overgrown, grabbing at her legs as the wind blew the blades onto her ankles - keeping hold of her this time. She looked at the concrete steps; the porch beckoned her. The stone pillars braced the deep colored bricks. The sky fell back, pushing the house closer. It wanted her. It waited for her.

"Go in, I'm here."

She swallowed hard, walked to the steps. The blades let go as they guided her forward. The decay in the air blew around her, circling her, pushing her inward. *I can't do this.* She felt like a child, helpless against its will.

"Go inside." she ordered.

Renee walked up the steps and put her hand on the knob. The door squeaked, echoing into the house. The house was dim, forsaken. She entered the living room. Her mother's thick wooden furniture filled the room. The dark paneling merged into the brown carpet. It was quiet. She walked into the dining room. The china cabinet stood in front of her, a table on the right. The dark paneling and carpet continued throughout the house.

"What do you see?"

Renee looked to the left. There was a small bathroom she remembered all too well. The circular indents on the door mocked her. The floor creaked when she lifted a foot to take a step. Frozen, she waited for the house to know she was there. Her heart raced, lungs stagnant, the clock on the dining room wall ticked continuously. She put her foot down, waited some more, looking all around her. Looking for what she sensed was there. Waiting, as she did so many nights in that house.

Another creak as Renee put her foot down and stopped in the bathroom. She looked in the mirror and saw her reflection. The reflection of herself when she was fifteen, so young and innocent; smooth skin, bright eyes. She walked out of the bathroom; on the left was her mother's room. Across from that was her baby brother's. Jack. She couldn't look in his room, not yet, maybe not ever.

The floor crackled and popped under her feet as she headed back toward the dining room. The clock ticked. Around the corner was the kitchen. Renee stopped right in the path of the door that led to the basement.

The basement she had spent her whole life trying to forget, now right in front of her, separated by only an inch of wood. The door seemed alive, begging her to open it and warning her at the same time to turn and run away. Her legs thickened, as tree trunks, so heavy that she could fall right through the floor and be immersed in the darkness.

"Tell me what you see." She heard the doctor say again as she stood staring at the door.

Renee's thoughts spun around her head. She's in a house from her childhood with all the knowledge of a thirty-five year old and she can hear the voice of her doctor as though it was God speaking directly to her, and all the while, she's terrified as if something could happen to her in a memory. "It's just like I remember it. I'm looking at the door to me and Lee's rooms, the door to the basement."

"Walk away from the door. It's not time."

The doctor's words were comforting as she backed away, never taking her eyes off it as she turned the corner. She stopped at the sound of giggling behind her. The room became blurred, she could barely see. She turned at the sound of the floor squeaking.

"Who's there?" she whimpered.

The giggling continued, light illuminated from the living room. Renee peeked around the corner and saw Lee sitting on the floor and Jack was sitting on her mother's lap in the chair next to him. Her mother was an alluring woman. Bronze skin, long straight black hair, big sad looking eyes, all traits she gave to the rest of the family. Except Jack. He had light blonde hair and an even lighter complexion.

"I see them." Renee said.

"Stop." the doctor said, turning on the light. "That was good." She sat back down in the chair. "Now I want you to go home, think about the house, think about your family. This will be hard but I want you to go visit them and we'll discuss that next time." she said.

Renee was in a daze walking out. *Go visit them? I can't, we haven't...*

The doctor called her name as she put her hand on the knob. "Before you go, can I ask one more question?"

Renee stopped the door halfway.

"What do you think was in that house?"

Silence filled every part of the room as she tried not to think of the answer.

"Renee?"

She turned her head to look the doctor in the eyes, like a child being forced to fess up, as a victim pointing out the assailant, and said, "Nothing. Absolutely nothing."

11

The leaves rustled around as she walked to the car. Dried up, dying, they reminded her of this town. She hates it here; everything is alike. She heard things were different when she was younger. The local factory employed most people. Couples went to dinner and the drive-in on Friday nights. When the plant closed lives seemed to close with it. The theater is a weed filled dump now with half the screen torn down. Fast food chains and bars line the main road with an occasional gas station to break up the scene.

She drove past an old couple walking down their steps, bundled up, somber looking. *Biding time. Looking for something better. It won't come, not here.*

She wandered the roads, unaware, until she reached the edge of town. A few miles farther than her usual travels, the buildings looked abandoned, dirtier than the others. *These should be condemned.* She thought after seeing a small girl walking through an alley littered with trash. She didn't know why she was here. The car continued forward to its destination, almost driving itself. She turned onto a side street, the car slowed, coasting by a two-story red brick building.

The concrete steps were cracked and falling apart just as the bricks on the exterior. Smashed aluminum beer cans were strewn about in front of the screen that hung on by only the bottom hinge. Renee turned the car off. It was familiar, *but why?*

Her gaze across the street was broken by a figure in the window quickly drawing the curtains closed. She could almost hear the screech of the hangers run violently across the rod as the curtain swayed back and forth.

Renee walked to the curb as the sky grew quiet. She seemed to shrink with each step she climbed up the porch. The air became thick, too thick to inhale. The smell of burning trash floated about. The porch grew longer, the steps wider.

Tap. Tap. Barely noticeable, the sound of the knock drowned out by the hustle of the wind.

"Hello?" she said turning the knob until the door opened to the slack of the chain. "Is anyone there?"

The door slammed shut on her face. The chain rattled and the door flew wide open. The room was empty; holes in the bottom of the walls, carpet crumpled up in knots throughout the room. A smell of urine and stale beer filled the desolate air.

"Hello?" she called out again walking through the living room.

She turned the corner into the kitchen. A woman stood crying at the counter with her back turned to her. Renee was overcome with sadness, emptiness; she knew the loneliness, the despair of this woman. "Are you alright?" she whispered.

"Why are you here?" the woman demanded.

Renee trembled, her stomach turned. She knew her voice, she did know. "Mom?"

The woman did not answer. Her crying stopped.

Renee's eyes filled, "Mom, is, is that you?"

The woman flung her head full force at Renee with fire in her eyes.

"Mom?" the woman mocked in a low voice with her teeth clenched together. "Why did you come here?" she scoffed as she stepped once toward Renee.

"Don't do this." she begged.

"Get out of my house, damn it! Get out!" Her mother squeezed her arm and drug her to the door, pointing to it the whole way.

"Mom please!"

"Please what? Please forgive you?"

"Forgive me?"

"Did he get a chance to beg?" she screamed as she pushed her through the door. "Don't ever come back!"

Renee ran to the car, fumbling with the keys, sobbing…the engine roared. "I didn't do it." The tires squealed as she sped through the whirlwind of leaves.

12

"Hey, hey! What's wrong?" Mike threw his arms around her.

"She blames me." she sobbed.

"It's alright." He held her tight until she calmed enough to sip some water.

"I want to lie down."

Mike sat on the couch and dropped his head in his hands as she went into the bedroom. He felt useless, shut out. Never knowing how to help her. Never knowing what to save her from. He loved her more than anything even after all these years. He knew he wouldn't let anyone hurt her but felt helpless to save her from herself.

He sat in the living room listening for her to scream, waiting for her to stagger through the house in a sleep walking daze. All he could do was be there when she woke up to tell her it was alright; nothing was there, he made sure of that. He checked on her as she slept on top of the covers with her clothes still on. He waited until he felt confident she would finally sleep through the night.

13

The roads in Littletin grew quieter as the evening settled in. Only a few cars sat in line at the drive-thru, the islands at the gas stations were deserted. Leaves tumbled top over bottom, almost running down the curb; hurrying on their way past the reach of the street lights. They followed the low autumn wind down the fields. Tree branches leaned in the same direction - pointing toward the outskirts of town. Black clouds blended with the sky, blocking the stars and moonlight. An overpowering wall of stillness pushed the rushing leaves into the air, creating a back turning funnel in the night just at the edge of the long driveway. The house sat impatiently.

Old Man Willie watched out his window. The lights dimmed at the nursing home where Ruth had been put in bed already. Melissa and Tom Dagen admired their treasures as they unpacked. Mike and the kids watched television in the downstairs family room.

14

Renee sat up in her bed, searching the shadowy room while her body was shaking and sweat gathered above her lip. Her heart pounded harder as she gasped through a cold, dense air. Her skin started to crawl with goose bumps. One at a time they crawled onto her legs, the smaller ones moving rapidly while the larger ones seemed to fall onto her skin like bricks. Together they walked in an uneven pattern up to her arms until she felt them on the top of her neck. That's when she knows they've covered her body, when they dance and multiply on top of each other as they run out of open breeding ground. She knew then she wasn't alone.

She didn't want to look around; she had to. The air felt thick as she took it in while the old musky smell tickled the start of her throat.

As the seconds seemed to stretch out into days, she started to calm a little. Maybe this time it will be okay. She looked to the door on the right. Her bedroom door that had tricked her so many times. She wanted to get up and run through it to see if it would lead out. It was surrounded by darkness that pushed her toward the center of the room. The tiny three bare walls closed inward.

The only thing she could move was her head as the rest of her body seemed sealed in a tomb of cement. She waited, with the covers held up to her neck. Waiting. *Tick, tick, tick...*

She closed her eyes and screamed so her mother would come save her. Loud and shrill. The never-ending, even-toned, high-pitched scream of a child. Even it scared her. When she opened her eyes, there she was, sitting in front of her, screaming back in her face.

Her dry and wrinkled skin was blotted with black and brown spots. Her teeth like wood from the decay. The smell permeating from her bones was unbearable. The smell of death as it sits in front of her and lingers in the air as it lightly touches her skin. Crawling on her like a cold fog, too thick to see through, so she can't tell what's making those sensations on her body. Like lanky, skinny fingers creeping up her leg; sucking the life out of her pores. Her hair was dingy gray with streaks of black showing through, as though it were once alive, now almost completely consumed by death.

Renee, still screaming, stares into the corpses eyes. It's the eyes that haunt her; the eyes prove to her that this lady, this thing, was something so much more than that. The eyes that stare back into hers have only one color and no pupil. The eyes she can see herself in and nothing else. The pitch black, shiny and new looking eyes are fixed on hers, like they're stealing her soul, with her mouth wide open and her sunken cheeks falling in toward her tongue while her cheek bones protrude under her eye sockets, never blink or stray off track. There they sat, both screaming at each other as though they would never stop.

With a jolt, Renee shot up out of her bed, still catching her breath, the smell lingering on her. She ran to flip the light on. She was home. *Just a dream, a dream, that's all.* Her mind raced. It's after eight; she had slept most of the evening. She went in the bathroom, her face looked old. *Disgusting!* She splashed water on it. *Crazy! Where are the kids? Dear God, they must be starved!* She went downstairs.

"There's pizza in the fridge." Mike grabbed her by the hand.

"No, I'm not hungry" she said, looking at the kids. *They can't know.* "I'll do the dishes."

It was just a dream. She thought as she washed and dried. The face stuck in her mind, the face she's seen most nights of her life, more vivid and alive this time.

Nicole came running up the stairs, through the kitchen.

"Stop running." Renee hollered as she put the pan in the strainer.

Her hair flowed through the air as she ran around the corner to her room.

"Hey!" she yelled again, heading through the living room. "I said stop running!" she scolded as she turned into Nicole's doorway.

"Who are you looking for?" Devin asked behind her.

Renee looked into the empty room. "Nicole, she was just here."

Devin looked at her, confused "But she's asleep on the couch downstairs."

Crazy! He knows. Don't let him see it!

Renee went back downstairs and sat next to Mike and Andrew. Mike put his arm around her pulling her close to him. She looked at Nicole as she slept peacefully on the couch. Devin came down the steps, watching his mother's face as he joined them.

15

"Did you visit your family?" Dr. Dagen asked.

Renee looked at her for a moment, silent, shaken, "No, not yet."

The doctor observed as Renee looked to the floor. *She's hiding something,* the doctor thought. "Alright." she said disappointed as she drew the curtains shut. "Lay down then."

The pillow looked soft, inviting. She had tossed and turned all night - to keep awake. She wanted to tell the doctor, she wanted someone to know. *Where would I start? How would it sound?* She was too tired to try. Like a drone, she did what she was told. She closed her eyes before the room went dark. The dream flashed in her mind, the corpse, screaming. This was the nightmare she had when she was forced to sleep in the basement. The water dripped from the pipes into puddles, footsteps pattered past her door; the whispering. *What did they say?* The doctor swung the light. Renee watched.

"Ten, nine, eight..."

She tried to look around, barely able to open her eyes. The walls had a thick cloudy fog around them. *Something's wrong,* she thought as a silhouette glided past her with a cool breeze. She squeezed her eyes together tightly to try to make the blur go away. Only streaks of colors in midair could be seen.

"Who is it?" the doctor asked. "Concentrate, stop blocking it and relax."

She jumped and looked in front of her as a door slammed shut. Small circles glowed from the door. Behind her, cabinets started opening and closing, silverware jangled violently as drawers opened and slammed shut.

Oh my God! I remember this!

"Stop it!" she yelled. Paralyzed.

Her heart pounded as the noises stopped. She knew where she was; she was in the dining room - in its path to the bathroom. "The bathroom." she whispered.

"Who's in the bathroom?" the doctor asked loudly as Renee heard the footsteps coming.

It was me. She thought as she looked down. "I am." she answered as she looked up; she was locked in the bathroom.

Tap and step. She heard that sound for the second time. *Tap and step.*

The footsteps stopped at the door, silence filled the house. Sweat dripped down her forehead and mixed with tears. "Don't do it, please." she cried to herself as she sat on the lid of the commode.

BANG! BANG! BANG!

She screamed with her face in her hands.

"Stop." the doctor took her hands. "Who was it?"

"They didn't know." Renee continued to sob. "The police came after I jumped out the window and went to the neighbor's house. They didn't find anyone else there."

"I think that's enough for today."

Renee tried to pull herself together as she went to the elevator. There wasn't much time before she had to pick Andrew up from practice and she couldn't be such a mess. The young doctor jotted down her notes.

16

Ruth wheeled through the dining room, wandering aimlessly as nurses prepared to get everyone ready for bed. Her chair jerked with each lunge as she propelled forward with both legs at the same time. Kitchen workers cleared the tables and hopped out of her path as she rolled by. Some were used to it, others sighed at the annoyance. "Na now now." she whispered to the floor.

She wheeled to the bedroom hallway. The main lights were out, only a shimmer of light shone at the top of the walls from the nightlights that had been placed over every other door. She turned into the anteroom. Her shadow stretched, filling the length of the long, darkened hall. Its head looked swollen from the helmet, the hair long and stringy. She leaned forward, causing the back on the figure to rise higher. There she stayed, leaving the vile shadow to guard the hall.

17

Nicole ran to her room and flung her bookbag on the bed. Renee sat at the table as the sun set on the early evening. She nodded, pulling herself awake. *Why does it have to get dark so early?* It would be the longest winter yet. The sporadic periods of rest weren't enough this year and it was early in the season, too early. *I'll never make it.* She wanted to hide in her shell where nothing could find her. She nodded again. Too much time had passed in the second she dozed. She called down the basement steps, "Devin, keep an eye on Nicole. I have to go get Andrew."

The air felt cold; she could see a white cloud as she exhaled. No time to warm the car, she couldn't be late again. She can't forget how scared he had been, so helpless in the middle of the universe with the night lit up by only a few stars that were closing in on him, about to swallow him whole.

It's five till six and she has just enough time. The car roared, scolding her as she backed out of the driveway. The images of the old house flashed through her mind. *I don't want to do this anymore.* The corpse screamed in her face.

A few blocks farther she noticed that no other cars were on the road. *Where is everyone?* The drive seemed long. The parking lot looked deserted. The lights were out in the building except one small yellowish-orange glow inside the doors.

"That can't be, I'm not late!"

She got out of the car. The sound of the door shutting echoed in the night.

"Hello?" she called out. She walked slowly up the sidewalk with her arms crossed to keep warm, looking to the sides and behind her. A cat yowled as a putrid smell crept up her nostril. She turned to get back in the car.

"Come on, answer." She slammed the phone shut. "Damn it!"

She started to drive to the highway when her phone rang at the stop sign.

"Where are you?" Mike asked. "Andrew called, he's waiting for you."

A line of cars passed in front of her. She turned around. *What's going on?*

Andrew was out front, all the lights were on. The parking lot was full of cars and parents were huddled on the sidewalk talking to each other.

"Where were you?" he asked, getting in the car.

Where was I? Her head pounded with dizziness. *I'm going crazy.*

18

Renee went to her room to change clothes. Her head throbbed with each step. She was confused, dazed. *Don't' let him see you like this. Stop it!* She sat on the bed. *It's just your mind playing tricks again.* She thought as she remembered her mother telling her that. She hated her room being in the basement of the old house. *It's just your mind playing tricks.* Her mother said each night when Renee would come running into her bedroom, begging to sleep on the couch. A few nights her mother gave in, allowing it, but always with the understanding that she couldn't keep doing it, keep running from it. She would eventually have to grow up and put those things out of her head. She fell back onto the bed, holding her head. *Tricks.*

"Mom was late again to pick me up!" Andrew said, slamming his bookbag on the kitchen table.

Mike closed the door to the fridge and saw the anger on Andrew's face.

"Can't you pick me up from now on?"

Mike walked to the table, motioning for Andrew to sit in the chair next to him. "Yes, I could, but I just walked in the door when you called so I would be late too if that's what you want."

Andrew dropped his head, running out of options.

"Mom's got a lot going on. She tries her best, you know that. I'm sure it was traffic or getting out of work late. Let's cut her some slack, okay?" he said, rubbing his hand over Andrew's head.

Andrew bobbed his head, reluctantly agreeing as he got up and followed Mike downstairs.

19

Mike listened as Renee stomped around upstairs. The bedroom door slammed, then the bathroom. He heard the kitchen cabinets fling and hit the doors next to them. *Clang!* The pot slammed on top of the stove.

Andrew looked up from his laptop. Nicole sat her homework on her leg. Devin looked at his dad. "She'll be alright." he said.

He wanted to believe his own words but he knew things weren't getting better, only worse. *She just needs to sleep,* he thought. If she could only sleep he would have his beautiful wife back; the kids, their vibrant mother. He hoped that the doctor would help. *Why didn't she give her medicine?*

Mike was a patient man - which he learned from his upbringing. His parents were strict Catholics. There would be no foul words, no cold heart and no running out on a marriage and family. *The hard times will determine how much of a man you are.* His father said that many nights when his mother had one of her fits. She was a good woman, who suffered from Schizophrenia. Most days were normal but the holes in the walls and the kitchen floor reminded him on the good days how bad the others could be.

"They're in there!" His mother screamed as she pried the kitchen tile up with a screwdriver; her eyes wild with fear.

His father knelt beside her. He stabbed at the floor with an ice pick, "We'll get them out!"

Mike watched as his father looked into his mother's eyes, touched her arm as he confirmed her feelings and calmed her completely by obliging her every whim. It worked on the kitchen floor just as it did with the bedroom wall and the ceiling by the attic. *I won't abandon her!* He loved Renee very much and would do whatever it took to help her, not that he ever dreamt of leaving.

20

"Devin." Renee called out.

He came upstairs with his pants sagging far enough that the top of his boxers were showing.

"Pull your pants up and set the table." she said, pouring noodles into the strainer.

"I'm playing a game mom. Can't Andrew or Nicole this time?" he begged.

Frustrated, exhausted. "They're doing homework. Your game will have to wait another three minutes."

He could tell by the look on her face that this wasn't an argument he would win.

"Time to eat." she yelled. The last bowl snatched out of her hands as she tried to set it on the table.

"How's the election going?" Mike asked.

"You're probably looking at the next President." Andrew smiled, tapping his chest with both hands.

"Good, I know you'll win." Renee said.

"Geek." Devin giggled.

"That's enough! Not at the dinner table." Renee snapped.

The table grew quiet, glances up at their mother, studying her face. The somber circles under her eyes were getting worse, her cheeks chiseled out. They could tell something was bothering her, something.

Renee felt drained by the time she cleaned up and did the dishes. The bed called her with a soft whisper. She popped two ibuprofen and flipped the bathroom light on. Her mind shut down as soon as her head hit the pillow.

"I'm sorry."

"I'm sorry."

She could hear the whispering of a child in her head.

"I'm sorry mom."

There were more voices now, speaking in unison. Her head spun, trying to wake from a much needed sleep.

"I'm sorry mom."

"I'm sorry."

The words kept coming and dragging her farther away from her slumber.

"I'm sorry."

Her head moving side to side.

"I'm sorry mom."

Her eyes started to adjust. As she awakened, she discovered it wasn't a dream.

"I'm sorry."

She focused, lifting her head. The kids were at the side of her bed looking down upon her. They whispered again as Renee sat up.

"I'm sorry mom."

"What, what are you sorry for?" she asked. There was no answer. Blank stares, still bodies. "What are you sorry about?" she demanded. She looked at the clock. *Tick, tick...*

She looked in the hall, then at them. She searched around their bodies, making sure they were alright. Nothing appeared to be wrong. She looked down at the floor and carefully back up, horrified by their uninhabited faces, the black eyes that stared into hers. She screamed and scooted to the other side of the bed, holding the covers up to her neck.

The light flipped on. Mike flew into the room, "What happened?"

Renee looked at him, shaking. She pointed to where the kids were.

"What?" he asked.

"They were there!" she screamed. *Floating off the ground!* She dared not to say.

"It was a dream Renee. There's no one there." he reassured her as he knelt on the bed.

"Where are the kids?" she demanded.

"Hopefully still asleep, it's two in the morning."

"I want to check on them, go with me."

He held Renee's hand as they went into the kids' bedrooms. They stood in the doorways until she was convinced they were asleep. Devin pulled the cover over his head when they left his room.

"It was a nightmare. Let's go back to bed."

"But I was awake." she said to herself as Mike turned her around and guided her to their bedroom. "I was awake."

21

Renee stayed awake through the night. She stared at the ceiling – she knew every little spot on the tiles. She knew how many tiles there were and how many lines, vertical and horizontal, how many boxes and triangles. She spent many nights counting and staring in her room. As the years passed, each night grew longer, running together exponentially. Sleep escaped her as the sun rose. Terrified, anguished to wake her kids. She had never dreamt of them before. She had never brought them into that realm of her life. *I have to protect them.*

Her night continued into the day; merging, inseparable. Her eyes tried to close at her desk. She pinched herself numerous times. She stuck a needle in her index finger until blood formed in a pool around it. By the end of the day the tips of her fingers were swollen and throbbing. Red tissues filled the trash can under her desk. Her papers had brown smears in the corners.

"Are you ready?"

Renee sat at her desk. *It's just your mind playing tricks.*

"Hey," Sharon put her hand on Renee's arm, "it's time to go. Are you ready?"

She started the car. *Get out of my house damn it! Get out!* She drove back to the edge of town. Her car stopped in front of the two story building. The windows were boarded up. *Don't ever come back!* She turned the car off and leaned back on the head rest.

Mike opened the door, watching each car that drove down the road. He paced; the kids, watching his every step.

"She didn't answer?" Devin asked.

Mike went to the door again. Her car pulled in the driveway. "Everything alright?" he asked, holding the screen open for her.

Renee walked in, unaware of his question. She saw the kids. "Bad day at work." she said as she walked into the kitchen.

Mike made dinner while Renee sat at the table. Keeping watch over her as he shuffled about. "You're tired Renee. I want you to take a sleeping pill tonight."

She nodded. The kids came in to sit down as Mike set the table. *They know.* She thought. They must know she's lost her mind. She needed them to feel safe. Mike spooned food onto her plate. Nicole looked at her mother and then at Andrew, they knew what each other was thinking.

"Is everything okay?" Renee asked her.

"Uh huh, are you?"

"Yes, eat your dinner." she put her head down to her plate.

The night seems to come fast as she looked out the kitchen window into the purplish sky. She knew the sun wouldn't be back for a long time; the rings were getting worse. She was tired and a full night of sleep was needed. She heard the distant sound of the dryer buzzer.

It's here. She thought as she watched the deep pink colors swirl around the sun as they pushed it into the ground. A mighty struggle, the blackness swallowing up the bright radiant sun. Her sun didn't win, it never does.

"Mom, I need my jeans with the pink ties going down the leg." Nicole yelled from her room.

"They'll be up in a minute." she yelled back as the blackness crept onto the earth.

Devin saw his mother in her room. "It's only eight-thirty, you goin' to bed?"

"I took a pill to help me sleep. I'm just tired, really tired. I'm alright though." She kissed his cheek, "I love you."

Satisfied that she would get some rest, he left her alone. "Love you too mom."

22

Old Man Willie sat in his rocking chair on the porch as he did every night. The country air was crisp; he zipped his plaid overcoat and lit his pipe. He watched up the rocked road as far as he could see until the white rocks and green weeds blended together in the dark. His house was second to the last on the dead end street. His radio played an old time banjo tune, fading in and out.

A car turned onto the road. The headlights lit up the cloud of dust as it drove down the way. A bass drum thumped through the metal of the car onto the ground. Old Willie grabbed his shotgun and strolled down his porch until he stood in the middle of the rocks. The car was still far off but he knew they could see him. He aimed his gun straight. The car stopped. A few miles still separated them. Old Willie squinted his right eye and spat. The car engine revved. The gun fired, echoing into the night. Birds flew out of the grass and trees, the car sped in reverse. Old Man Willie strolled back up his porch and sat down, lighting his pipe.

23

Renee's eyes drifted. She fought back, never letting them close all the way. She tried to count the tiles but couldn't keep focused. The light shone through the hallway, comforting her. She wished she hadn't taken that pill. She wished she hadn't gone back to that building. Her lids closed. She tried to open them, terrified that she would lose. *I should get up.* She thought. *I should...*

She opened her eyes, it was pitch black. *The bathroom light is out!* She couldn't breathe. She ran to the living room. The silhouettes of Nicole in the recliner and Mike asleep on the couch could be seen by the fuzzy light of the television. She fumbled to the light switch.

I have to turn the light on. She thought, desperately trying to reach it. She flipped the switch up; nothing happened. The startle of the unexpected continued darkness woke her.

She sat up, darkness filled the house. She jumped out of bed and looked at Nicole in the recliner and Mike on the couch as she ran to the switch.

Again she awoke after flipping the switch. She jumped out of bed, looked around the living room to the same scenario while running to the switch. She quickly flipped it and when the light didn't come on she ran to the bedroom. She saw herself asleep on the bed, frantically she reached down to grab her arm and in a deep voice sounding in slow motion yelled, "Get up!"

She fell into the doorframe. Her body lunged forward into the living room and when she turned the corner she saw Nicole in the recliner and Mike asleep on the couch. She fell side to side into the walls as she tried to get to the light switch. She almost reached it.

"Mom, what's wrong?"

She kept going, focusing on her goal. She had to see if the light would come on and end this cycle.

"Mom," Nicole shrieked, frightened, as she started to stand, "what's wrong?"

Renee stopped, looked at her daughter and knew she was really awake. She fell onto the recliner and put her head on Nicole's lap.

"What is it?" she asked, stroking her mother's hair.

She looked up, almost starting to tell her, "Just a dream."

Renee slept on Nicole's lap, unable to fight it anymore. Nicole sat in the chair waiting for her to get up. It frightened her to see her mother this way. Mike woke and lifted Nicole from under Renee and carried her to her room.

"What's wrong with mom?" she whimpered.

Mike tucked her in bed. "Mommy's just tired." he said as he kissed her goodnight.

Mike covered Renee in the recliner. *How do I help you?* He wondered as he pushed strands of hair off her face. He went back to the couch.

Renee woke in the morning, confused. She put the cover back on their bed and went downstairs. The kids were awake already. *Don't let them see.*

Devin put his game on pause. "Nicole said you had a nightmare last night?"

"Yeah." she said, trying to shrug it off.

"She said you looked like you were drunk or something."

She laughed, "No, I wasn't awake all the way. Must've been the pill." She straightened the cushions on the couch.

He looked down, trying to decide if the answer would be good enough. He started to walk away and then turned. "She said you looked weird, like you were being dragged around."

24

Melissa stopped picking up the dirty dishes off the dining room table to admire the chandelier they had found at an antique shop on Broadway after work yesterday. It fit the Victorian-style perfectly. Tom installed it, with the help of some friends, as soon as they woke this morning. She looked all around, admiring the rest of the room. She was pleased that they finished in time for their house warming party.

"It's still early if you wanna do something." Tom said as he closed the door on the last guest. "We could get dressed up and go to The Little Theater downtown."

"No, I want to stay in. I'm not done taking it all in." she said.

They finished clearing the table and went into the kitchen to wash the dishes.

"How's work coming along, any crazies yet?" Tom flinched, waiting for her to fling him with the towel.

"That is not nice!" she said, trying to stop from smiling. "Actually, the best thing going right now is a lady who has trouble sleeping, nightmares." She shrugged her shoulders.

"Sounds boring." he joked as he continued to wash the dishes and hand them to her.

Melissa dried the ceramic plate and carefully placed it in the rack under the cupboard. "Well, there's more. She hasn't seen her family in a really long time." she paused, "but I don't know why yet." She grabbed another plate from him. "Still kinda boring." she laughed.

"Just wait, you'll be begging for cases like that in a month or two."

Melissa thought about all the years she spent preparing for the day she would have her own practice. She dreamt of helping people since she was a little girl. She was always the one her friends told their problems to, real problems, tangible issues. "I can only hope!" she said.

25

Devin walked into Andrew's room and sat on the bed. Andrew glanced up from his laptop, scooting over to make room. "What do you want?"

Devin looked down at the covers.

"What's wrong?" Andrew asked.

Devin shrugged his shoulders, picking at the sheet. Andrew put his laptop in front of him. "Did you get in trouble or something?"

"It's mom." he said. "Were you awake the other night when she came in our rooms?"

Andrew pursed his lips, "No, when?"

Devin dropped his head, "Doesn't matter." He started to get up.

"I know she's been late to pick me up a few times. Gettin' really mad about that!"

Devin sat back down. "Nicole was really upset when mom came in the living room last night. She was crying when she told me about it."

"She's too sensitive, makes a big deal out of little stuff. Mom's always been like that."

"Yeah." he said, getting up to go in the hall. "You're right."

Andrew put the laptop back across his legs.

26

It's Sunday morning and Renee felt weighted down. Her body was heavy, arms and legs a burden that she had to lug around. Getting out of bed seemed almost impossible.

"Come on mom." Andrew hollered in the doorway to her room. "We're gonna be late!"

"A few more minutes." she slurred.

She could hear the kids telling Mike she wouldn't get up. She could picture his response. Nodding his head and waiving his hand downward to tell them to calm down, he would take care of it.

"Renee?" Mike whispered.

"What?"

"Are you going to church today?"

"I'm trying." She didn't want to go. She had only been asleep a few hours. She could stay there all day.

He chuckled, took her hand to pull her up. "Come on, you'll feel better after seeing Pastor Dave. You always do."

She went unsteadily to the closet and took the first thing she saw. Mike sighed, head hung down as he walked out of the room.

At least I'm going.

As Mike drove, Renee leaned on the window, watching the passing cars in the sunlight; wondering how their lives must be. They parked and walked up the sidewalk to the church. Renee counted the steps. *Twenty-four, twenty-five, twenty-six...* The church bell rang breaking the sequence. Her gaze went up to the bricks. The tan vertical lines disappeared in the blue sky.

"Good morning Mike." Pastor Dave said as Renee stood a short distance away, looking up into the heavens. Gray clouds shifted in, overtaking the white, cool-whip shapes in the sky.

Thirty-one, thirty-two... She counted up to the entrance. The sky turned completely gray as the bricks seemed to darken themselves. She stopped to watch families enter.

"Come on Renee." Mike said curiously.

"It's not right." she mumbled.

Inside, everyone was in place. All was as it should be. Grandma and Aunt Gladys were sitting close on the right side, with their hair high in the air. The translator was on the left looking ready to bounce. Pastor went up front, praying to himself. Everything was right yet felt so wrong.

The family sat in the middle pews. The words swirled in her ears while she hung her head to the floor. Once in a while she heard shouts of "Amen". Nothing else held her attention. The nod of her head awakened her enough to sit up straighter and compose herself. She tugged the bottom of her shirt down and swiped the front of it; lifting her head up to look like she had been paying attention.

The people sitting in front of her were all turned, facing her. She froze, wondering if Pastor asked a question of her. She looked left, then right. Everyone was turned in her direction, eyes fixed.

Their eyes stopped her heart. The big, black eyes they all shared as one. Vacuous, lifeless faces.

"Renee, you okay?" Mike nudged her arm.

She looked at him, comforted by his blue eyes.

"You're shaking."

"I'm not feeling well." she said, searching around the room to see everyone looking straight ahead.

"I shouldn't have made you come. Let's go home."

"Mom?" Nicole asked from the back seat. "What does faith mean?"

Nothing came to her. *How can I teach her something I'm losing?*

"Faith is knowing that no matter what choice you make, it will be the right one. God will make sure of that." Mike looked at Renee, disappointed that she didn't answer.

She rested her head against the window again.

27

"I would ask how you are, but you look terrible." Dr. Dagen said as Renee went to the couch. "It's only Monday. Are you going to make it the rest of the week?"

"I'm not sleeping well."

"Maybe you should take some time off work."

That won't help. Nothing will help.

"Do you want to continue today?"

Renee looked at her. *I don't have a choice.* She looked at the couch. "It doesn't matter."

The doctor studied her face, her actions. Renee's demeanor has changed, she wrote it on her notepad. "Did something happen since our last meeting?"

Renee stood in front of her. "Just more dreams."

More dreams. The doctor thought. *How do I stop these dreams if she won't let me in?* The doctor was certain her mother was the answer. *How do I get her to see her family? Or even talk about them?*

"Okay, lie down and we'll get started then." she sighed, darkening the room.

Renee wiped the tears welling up in the corners of her eyes. She put her head on the pillow, squeezing her face tight. Dr. Dagen sat in the chair, pulling it closer to the couch. The room seemed quieter to her as she clicked the pen light on. She held the light upside down, starting to swing it. Renee unclenched her face and stared into the beam of light. The doctor looked behind her as the room appeared to darken even more. She heard the tick of the clock above her desk. The light continued to swing. Dr. Dagen turned around and started to count.

Renee's eyes started to drift. She opened them, still lying on the couch in the dark. She gasped for air, she was alone, unable to move. All she could do was wait. Wait until the night was through playing hide and seek and show her what it wanted this time. Wait for another eternity for the ending she knew would come.

Time slowed and the longer it takes, the more terrified she becomes. She tried to envision something else, a carnival, school, anything else. The dryness in her eyes turned to a steady burn as they begged for her to blink.

I can't, that's when they trick you.

She thought of her Grandma and going to church with her on Easter. She imagines herself in the little white lacey dress and matching tights. She remembers sitting in the basement classroom of the children's church. The faces of the other kids and the teacher are a blur; their voices mimic a deep, jumbled up man's voice, like a recording playing in slow motion. She tried to remember a prayer she taught her although it doesn't come.

"Now I lay me down to sleep. I pray the Lord my soul to keep." She whispered to herself, lips barely moving. "If I shall die before I wake, I pray the Lord my soul to take." The words coming slower now as she got to the dying part.

"Jesus loves me this I know, for the bible tells me so." *Yes, this is better.* She remembered. This was the song she sang. This was what helped her stay in her room. "Little ones to him belong. They are weak but he is strong."

The pressure eased as she sang it again and again. The words soothed her as she sang. The tension lifted and she closed her eyes.

Ahhh. The fire instantly put out when her eyes started to water. She opened them after singing for the fourth time. She lifted her eyes up to her eyebrows and slightly tilted her head up.

She froze. She started to scream as she looked at Lee hovering over her, bent down with his face an inch in front of hers. His face was hard looking, like the plastic head of a doll. He lowered his jaw, farther and wider than humanly possible. "Stop." he said in the same deep man's voice playing in slow motion that she heard come from the mouth of the Sunday school teacher.

Renee jumped up from the couch, stomping in place like a baby while her arms were waving about, screaming. Arms gripped all around her, with a downward pushing force, attacking her. She swung without looking and heard a familiar voice ordering, then begging her to stop.

"That's enough!" Dr. Dagen yelled as she let go.

Renee broke down and fell to the floor sobbing.

The doctor sat quietly, taking it all in. "Why are you afraid of Lee?"

Confused, dazed, Renee wondered why she would ask that. "Lee was the only one there for me," she paused, "he was always there for me."

"Then what happened there? You'll have to face it sometime!"

Renee sat on the couch, wiping her face with her fingers as she looked away from the doctor.

"Why don't you take the rest of the time to get some sleep, you look like hell."

Renee laid her head down while the doctor wrote at her desk. Her eyes closed readily, sleeping better than she had in a week.

After Renee left, Dr. Dagen sat at her desk listening to recordings and reviewing notes she'd taken of their sessions. She feels like she's failing, not only herself but Renee as well. *She's never going to open up to me.* She knew what she had to do. It would be best for both of them.

"Hi honey, listen I'm gonna be a little late tonight. Have to make a quick stop, shouldn't be but an hour." Grabbing her purse and keys she locked up the office. Her phone was open to the GPS application. She read the directions. It was only a twelve minute drive to Pine Street.

28

Devin waited for his mother to get home. He wanted desperately to help her. He knew she tried hard not to let them see what she was going through. Andrew and Nicole noticed it but didn't think much of it. It was normal for them, the way she's always been.

He listened for her car to pull up. He wanted to tell her he was sorry for what he said. He wanted her to know how much he loved her and that she was a good mother.

She finally came home. He threw his arms around her and tried to speak.

"Shh." she said. He didn't need to say anything, she knew.

29

Dr. Dagen followed the directions on her phone. The houses became farther in between on the lower class edge of town. Her car swerved to miss the holes in the road. She pulled onto the long rocked driveway. *It's horrible.* She thought of the abandoned pile of bricks. The lifestyle she was accustomed to wouldn't let her imagine how anyone could live there. *Poor little Renee.* She thought, opening her car door. The wind picked up, blowing against her as she tried to make her way through the yard. *They're only dreams, a little girl's dreams.* She tried to convince herself as she felt uneasy, alone. The tree creaked, threatening to fall over in front of her as the branches swayed in the air like arms reaching down upon her. She held her purse and keys tight, reaching the steps. She pinched her nose closed against the stench that worsened the closer she came to the house.

"I wouldn't go there if I was you."

She turned, an elderly man dressed in blue jean overalls and a sun-faded red Cardinals baseball hat was standing at the side of the house.

"And why is that?" she asked.

The man shuffled to her, surveyed his way down her silk top and tight fitted khaki skirt to her high heeled pumps. "A purdy lady like you shouldn't be messin' with a place like this. Only ones that try an' go there now are the crazy teenagers. I keep them out though."

She took a step back, unnerved by his manner. "I know someone who lived here, a long time ago. I just wanted to see if for myself."

He laughed. "It had to be a long time ago. Ain't no one lived here for 'bout twenty years now. E're once in a while some kids will try to have a party on the weekend but I run them off. Nobody wants to live here. Whole town knows what happened."

Dr. Dagen smiled, "Well I'm new in town. Mind tellin' me what happened?"

He looked down, took the pipe out of his mouth and glided his eyes back up her body. "There's been a lot of death in that house. It's no good. That's why I ain't lettin' you in."

Dr. Dagen looked back at the house, her smile receding. "Alright, I thank you for your time sir." she said as she backed away to her car.

What did he mean by that? She opened her laptop and typed "**Pine Street Littletin, Illinois**". She scrolled through an endless array of houses for sale. Nothing more matched her query.

30

"Good morning." Sharon said.

Renee gave her a sideways glance.

"Okay, it's another one of those days, huh?"

Renee went to her desk. It felt good to be at work, normal. It was quiet, the phone barely rang, Sharon hardly spoke.

Ruth came in head first. Sharon and Renee prepared to block her from taking things off their desks. "Here we go again." Sharon laughed.

Ruth wheeled up to Sharon's desk. She didn't try to take anything this time. She picked at her shirt instead. Renee turned her chair around and rolled it over to the other corner behind the desk. She thought it would be easier if they double-teamed her. Renee could watch the left side and Sharon, the right.

"I jammed the copier across the hall." A nurse said as she poked her head in the office.

"I'll go." Sharon said as she got up to go fix it. "You watch her."

Renee wheeled her chair to the center of the desk to have full reach of all sides. Sharon was gone for a while and Ruth started to pluck. Renee put her left hand on top of the papers when Ruth reached for something on the other side. Renee put her right hand over that pile and noticed that her hands were spread out; resembling Pastor Dave's when he's preaching. She looked at Ruth and remembered what he said.

I cast you out in the name of Jesus. Leave this body at once in Jesus' name. Amen. She thought to herself.

"I'm not ready to go."

Renee heard those words and looked to see who was there. No one. Only Ruth. She looked at her and for the first time Ruth stared Renee right in the eyes; with clarity, with conviction. "I'm not ready to go." Ruth said, as lucid as could be.

Renee pushed herself backwards in the rolling chair as far away from her as possible. Ruth looked down and stole some papers with that faraway look that was somehow comforting.

Sharon came in and took the papers from Ruth and wheeled her out.

What the hell just happened? She couldn't have known what I said in my head!

Sharon sat down. Renee snapped out of it.

"What's wrong with you?"

"I don't know." she said, "I think I need to go home."

31

"There's been a lot of death in that house."

Dr. Dagen couldn't get what the old man said out of her head. She needed to find out what he meant if she would ever be able to help. Renee was keeping something from her, she was sure of that and she was going to find out what it was.

"Can I help you?"

"Yes, I want to find some information about the history of a house here in town. Can you show me where to look?"

The librarian smiled sarcastically, "Well, you can find just about anything on the internet. Do you need help using it?"

Dr. Dagen took a deep breath, making sure not to upset the person who might be able to help her. "I did try that, to no avail I'm afraid."

"Hmm, that is odd. What house are you looking into?"

"It's an old house, on Pine Street."

The woman paused. "I see, the old Foller place I assume? No one ever asks about any other house on that street."

"Yes. How did you know?"

She walked toward the computers. "You can't find anything about it because nothing has happened since the city changed its name." She gestured for the doctor to sit. "It used to be Willows, when the Foller's lived there. They changed it in 1988. After what happened." She typed "Willows Street Littletin, Illinois".

"I see. Thank you very much." Dr. Dagen said.

There were many newspaper articles. All of them about the Foller's on Willows Street. Dr. Dagen read one, then the next and the next. Marie Foller, Renee Foller, Jack Foller. Each article said the same thing. She read a few more.

"Oh my God." She jumped up and ran to her car.

"Hi, this is Dr. Dagen. I have a practice here in town and I need birth and death records. Yes, yes. Tomorrow's fine."

32

The drive to work the next morning seemed to take forever, giving her plenty of time to think. Think about what was happening. Everything was blurring together. Nowhere felt safe.

How did this all start? She asked herself, not sure if it ever really ended since she ran from the house.

She parked her car in the usual spot and looked at herself in the mirror. She watched as co-workers shuffled into the glass doors surrounded by red brick.

Ruth, how could I face Ruth? Her hands dropped as she started to cry. She looked at the building; it almost seemed to breathe as each red brick gradually turned to a coffee color, appearing to be alive and ready for her to come in.

"I can't do this." she cried out as she started the car and backed out.

Tears poured as the car headed to church. She needed to talk to Pastor Dave. She opened the car door before she changed her mind. She went inside to an empty chapel. Loneliness crept inside as she walked up the velvet aisle. She rubbed her hand on the mahogany wood of each pew. Walking toward the front, she remembered a lifetime here. She sat down in the front row to look at the murals on the ceiling.

"Renee?"

"Grandma?" she smiled as she stretched her arms out.

She kissed her on the cheek, "Just precious."

A secure feeling of long ago came over her as she felt the smile on her face.

"Are you off work today?" Realizing it was Wednesday.

"I didn't feel like going in."

She sat down next to Renee and sighed. "They're fascinating, aren't they?"

Renee followed her gaze up to the murals. "Yeah, they really are."

"You know, you don't have to be here to be near him."

"I know, but it sure seems like it sometimes."

"It's not your fault, nothing you can do can bring him back." She put her arm around Renee's shoulder and smiled again. "Just have faith."

Faith. That word again. The word she couldn't explain to her daughter. The word she thought she understood until she actually needed it. *Faith*

Renee kissed her grandmother goodbye and went home to call work to take a couple of days off.

33

Dr. Dagen was consumed by the need to help Renee. She waited impatiently at the Vital Records Department.

Come on. Come on!

"May I help you?" the tall, slender woman asked.

"I'm Dr. Dagen. I'm here for the records I ordered yesterday." she fidgeted.

The woman searched on top of the desk, picking up stacks of paper that were organized by some kind of logic. "Hmm." she sighed as she looked in the cabinets below the desk. "Ah, here we go."

"Thank you, thanks so much!" Dr. Dagen ripped the top of the manila envelope as she walked out of the building. She stopped on the steps outside.

What?

She fumbled in her purse. "Renee, this is Dr. Dagen. I was really hoping to reach you. I'll see you at your appointment tomorrow. It's very important that you come, don't be late!" she slammed the phone shut.

34

The house was quiet with Mike at work and the kids at school. Renee went to her room and pulled the curtains to let all the day's light in. She curled up on the bed. She felt confident in the sunlight as she glanced around the room. She wrapped up in the cover.

She slept deeply and dreamt of a bright and sunny day in the park. The kids were there, only younger, playing on the swings and slides. She pushed Nicole's swing while she laughed and giggled. Devin and Andrew chased each other around the playground.

"Mom, come get me." Andrew called out, running towards a tunnel.

She chased after him, laughing. She came to the opening of the tunnel he went into and turned to look at Nicole, squinting to see past the sunlight. She turned around and ducked her head to go in, following Andrew's laughter. As soon as she put her last foot in, the sunlight dissipated, the laughter stopped and she was trapped in a tomb of darkness.

It was damp and murky and there wasn't much room as the walls appeared to narrow. The farthest thing from her mind was to continue on and discover what's ahead. To find out what was making that foul, rotted smell. Noises came from ahead, like a cat trapped, moaning high and low in the near distance. She tried to see behind her, the side; it was completely black. She couldn't make out her hand in front of her face. She stretched her arms out on both sides and felt the cold, wet feel of dirt, *clay?* Turning as she dug her nails in to find a way out, any way except straight ahead. She was distraught, overwhelmed as she thought she had been buried alive. She had to get out. There was no other way.

She kept her arms up to search along the wall. Cautiously she put one foot in front and nearly twisted her ankle on the unsteady ground below. She felt around with her other foot, she could tell that she was stepping on rocks or a stone walkway of some kind. Her foot sloshed in the water around the stones. Old pipes ran across the top of the tunnel, water dripped from them into the puddles below. Footsteps ran past the sides of her, giggling, whispering. "Do it Renee."

What are they saying? She kept going, careful not to fall on the moving ground.

The noises grew louder with every step. The howling and moaning were making her head spin and she had to stop. Stop because of the awful, the wretched and horribly awful smell. She had to bend over violently and vomit at the rotted flesh smell.

She stood up, wiping her mouth with her wrist and held her hands over her mouth and nose. She took a few steps more while she held her face in her hands, not caring any longer about feeling her way. She had to keep that stench from creeping up her nose and entering her body. She walked ahead, feeling a warm breeze by her ear. She turned; it's all around her now.

A light! Straight ahead! She saw a small yellowish-orange light. *That must be the way out!*

Faster now, she was going faster now to get to the light. She had to know where she was. The more she went on, the farther she felt from the angelic light. Tears ran down her face as she felt trapped in a fun house maze.

I have to get out of here!

The noises were louder still and the breeze, that breeze with the smell in it. She was running. Her feet were turning sideways as she ran on the stones and missed most of them. Water splashed up in the air as she ran and cried.

Then, something touched her thigh. She stopped. Afraid if she moved it would know she's still there. It touched her again; fingers on her leg, with long nails, scratching down the length of her body. She cried out in agony as she felt the gashes in her skin, tearing and shredding her flesh as she took hold of herself and tried to hide in the wrap of her own arms.

She looked ahead and appeared much closer to the light now. There's an expanded room there. She could tell she was in some kind of cave.

I can make it!

A long, skinny, blackened arm stretched out from the side of the cave, just in front of her wide, glowing room. More of the enclosed was lit up now and uncovered what was lurking.

She saw, one at a time, what had been making those noises. Their faces were that of dirt covered, fleshy skeletons. They surrounded her. All along the way, she saw them now as they maneuvered somewhat robotically. Their arms were elongated, with stringy, slimy weeds hanging off of them. They were naked and grayish-brown, with their bones showing through their torsos. Their knees were bent and their backs were hunched up in the air while their enormous heads flung backwards as they stretched their mouths to let out those blood curdling moans.

Renee was surrounded; behind her, the sides, everywhere except straight ahead. They were leading her. She had to keep going, there's no other choice. As she cried, they closed in on her; on her neck, by her ear, at her feet, in front of her face. Moaning their breath over her skin and scratching. Blood dripped from her arms, stomach and legs. That ungodly smell, everywhere.

As the cave lit up more with each step, she realized that she's seen these things before. Their hair, dirty gray down their backs; their teeth, wooden and sharp; the eyes, soulless, yet united as one. These were her demons.

She ran until she entered the room and stopped suddenly. There stood their master. Master is all she could think of to call it. It was the same as the others only taller, thicker and more evil looking that anything she could imagine. It looked her in the eyes and flung its head back and howled. Behind it were three tall doors. The wet dirt covered the front of them, sliding down to the ground. She knew, somehow, what she had to do.

She must choose one. A door that either led to her freedom, her salvation, heaven? *Am I dead?* Or another that led to an eternity in the pits of their stomachs. She had to choose, it's the only way out.

What if I'm wrong? Tears streamed down her face.

"No," she whispered, "..no, NO!" she shouted and the howling all the length of the cave did not like her voice. She thought of her daughter in the back seat, her grandmother at the church, then of Mike.

The howling was loud and pierced through her head as she covered her ears with both hands and fell to her knees. They sank in the muddy water puddles as she lifted her head up, sobbing, looking right into the eyes of the beast. A new feeling came over her.

She felt an overwhelming peace as she knew it didn't matter. She stopped crying. She rose to her feet keeping her eyes on the master. Peace. The beautiful feeling of knowing. Of realizing. It doesn't matter.

"It doesn't matter." she smirked and the master howled louder than before. "It doesn't matter which one I choose." she said.

They all were howling and backing away from her. She was in control and an overwhelming peace replaced her fears. The room turned to a bright yellow as she went up to a door, any door, eyes closed, and pushed it. She turned to look at the giant as it lunged at her yet stopped suddenly.

"It doesn't matter." she said, walking through the warm, blinding light. The warmth subsided, the light softened, her eyes focused; she was in her bed – the sheets stained with mud.

35

Melissa came out of the bathroom and climbed into bed. Tom put a piece of paper in his book and closed it, setting it on the nightstand. He reached over to put his arm around her with a devilish smile. "How's my girl tonight?" he teased.

She nudged him aside.

"What's wrong?"

Melissa scooted closer to him, "Just hold me."

Tom wrapped her in his arms tight. "No problem there." he whispered. "What's going on?"

She didn't answer. She kept seeing the papers she read. Her confidence as a doctor was challenged. Unsure if she was ready to take on such a case. Unsure if she was even capable of helping Renee.

Tom squeezed tighter, "You don't want to talk about it?" he asked. "Did I do something?"

She put her arms around him. "It's not you. I'm not sure what it is yet." She smiled, "You were right about one thing though, I'm begging for the insomniac back."

He kissed her forehead. "You can do it. It's what you've been waiting for." he said as he twisted the switch on the lamp.

36

Dr. Dagen spoke into her recorder. "I'm going to try Reality Therapy today during the hypnosis. It will make her or break her." She clicked it off as Renee entered the room. "I hope you're ready for this." the doctor said, closing the curtains nervously.

She was. She really was. She wasn't afraid. She felt ready. The time has come that she faces her fears. She didn't know why this was happening to her; she now knew that she was going to end it. No matter what, it would end. "Ready."

The doctor flipped the light off and sat in front of her. *She's so brave.* She thought of her doctor as the pen light swung back and forth. She was ready for that.

She opened her eyes, standing in the door to the living room. It was just as it was before. Her mom and Jack were sitting in the chair, Lee on the floor. Something's different this time though. None of them were moving, not even baby Jack. Black bands under their eyes, the same barren expressions on their faces. She stayed as motionless as they were.

At once, they turned their heads to her. She went into the room and knelt down beside the chair. Those cold vacant stares; soulless. She looked over at Lee who was sitting up at her side, breathing on her neck.

"Where's Lee?" the doctor asked.

"He's here, with mom and Jack." She stared into his eyes.

"Renee, listen to me. Who is Lee?"

Renee sat in front of him.

"Listen very carefully. You never had an older brother. There's no record of him at all, anywhere."

Renee looked back at her mother, then at Lee. The skin started to bubble on his face, sliding off into a puddle of wax on the floor.

"No." she cried. "That can't be. He was always with me."

She stood up, gulped down, and went through the dining room into the kitchen to the basement door. This door that continued to call her to come through. She put her hand on the doorknob, turning it. She heard screaming howls on the steps as she unsealed it. The steps were gloomy with the same rotting smell. Jack was standing on the top step.

"Where's Jack?" she asked.

Renee cried, "On the steps."

"Did you kill him?"

"No!" she yelled as she looked next to him and saw herself, herself at fifteen, push him.

Jack's screams stopped with a thud. The young Renee looked back at her with a smirk and vanished. She wanted to run after him though her legs wouldn't allow it.

"Your mother Renee, what did you tell me about your mother?"

Renee sobbed, dropping to her knees.

"Renee?"

"She still blames me." she whispered.

"Renee, your mother killed herself in that house after Jack died. That's why you moved out so young. Your mother has been dead for twenty years."

Crazy! They knew you were crazy! "No!" *You're gonna be locked away. Your kids are in danger!* "No!"

Pain shot through her foot as she put it on the first step. Not a pain that she was used to, it was agony. She felt tortured and alone. Another step brought more of the same. The descent down each step felt terrifying. Hands clutched at her through the walls that were covered in dirt.

Jesus loves me this I know. She sang to herself until she reached the bottom and saw Jack's still body.

"You made me do it!" she yelled at the house.

She poked her head into the basement; it was darker than black. She couldn't see anything; the noises stopped. As she turned the corner, next to her bedroom door she tried to see down the hallway. The darkness shifted; moving silently in front of the room that she remembered as Lee's. *Who was down here with me all this time?*

Her mind raced. Her eyes focused enough to make out the outline of someone looking down in the doorway.

"Who's there?"

The figure raised its head.

"Stop." she whispered, still the image kept moving. "Stop. Dr. Dagen say stop." she cried out.

Run, damn you, run!

She felt her heart racing as her body geared up to take off. She looked behind her as the office intertwined with the house. The ticking was louder than ever as it filled the basement.

"Stop!" Dr. Dagen yelled as Renee's body flailed about on the couch. The lights in her office flickered on and off and a steady breeze threw her papers about as she cowered down to the floor and crawled behind the couch, peeking up over the arm.

Renee was still there. The figure's head rose all the way up now and opened its eyes. Beaming bright red, they cast a light over his body. It was Lee. She remembered him. Alone in her room, afraid to run upstairs. He came to her. She remembered years of being with him. Never speaking a word. He always came after the footsteps stopped, after the whispering. He stood in her doorway, looking down at her. Not a word.

They're tricking you. Run! She thought and turned her head around and saw the doctor looking at them from behind the couch. *Run!* She looked back at this thing, *what are you?*

"What are you?" Her voice getting louder with each word. "What are you?" She looked at her hands, they were older, her hands. She was taller, she was really there.

With all her might she wanted to run up the steps and lock the door. She didn't. She looked at this thing and stood up straight. *I'm not that person anymore.*

The figure started to make a deep noise. The farther its jaw lowered, the louder it became.

"I'm not afraid."

As soon as his body rose up into the air and twisted, it became the old lady from Renee's nightmares. She flew at her with her hands reaching out.

"I'm not afraid!"

She grabbed hold of Renee's throat as she finished her words. She wrapped herself around Renee as she flew laps around her body. With each lap, their eyes would lock for a moment. Renee's body tightened creating a barricade from letting her in. Those black eyes, evil and soulless. She stared into them not scared, not screaming, not running. She stood perfectly still, unafraid.

Each time she went around, she became more transparent until she eventually disappeared. The basement brightened and Renee saw sunlight glistening through the windows. She turned to go to the stairs. Dr. Dagen perched on the floor in front of the last step. Her breath coming fast, almost hyperventilating. Renee rushed to calm her. She looked up at Renee with windblown hair and her glasses falling of her face as Renee helped her up the stairs.

The house looked bright. The air light, somewhat fresh. She called a cab as they went down the front steps and into the yard to wait. Neither of them said a word as they waited and Renee knew she would never see the doctor again.

The old man lurked at the side of the house. He shook his head at the doctor and backed out of sight after seeing Renee.

As they waited for a ride to the office, Renee looked at the house that had haunted her all of these years. The helplessness was gone, she wasn't afraid anymore. *It's over.* She thought as she took a final look before getting into the cab. *It's all over.*

37

Devin was home alone playing a video game as he usually did after school. He was just about to beat the game that he'd been playing for about three weeks now when he heard his mom calling him.

"Hang on, I'm almost done." he yelled as he pushed the button on the controller as fast and as hard as he could. Just one more bar of the enemies' life left and he couldn't stop now.

"Come here." he heard her say again. He took his eyes off the game for a second to answer her and somehow it got behind him and killed his guy. Disgusted, he rolled up the controller and turned the game off.

"What?" he hollered as he walked out of the family room. There was no answer. He searched the entire basement. "Mom?" he yelled as he went up the stairs. He looked in every room. He was alone.

38

Renee and the doctor rode in silence, looking out opposite windows. They passed by the boarded up, abandoned apartment building she saw her mother in. *I lived there.* She remembered. Her mother couldn't go on after finding Jack's body and Renee sitting in the empty room at the end of the basement. Her mother knew something wasn't right but was in complete despair. She went upstairs and took all the pills she could find in the cabinet and went to her bed. Renee sat in the empty room through the night, in a trance. The next morning she couldn't wake her mother after seeing Jack's body on the basement floor, so she ran. The apartment building is where she ended up, alone until Mike saved her. It all came so vividly to her now. Was Lee someone she made up when she was younger so she wasn't always alone or was he a demon who had tricked her, convinced her he was real? She would never know. She only knew that it was over.

After they arrived at the office building, Renee stopped at her car to take a last look at her doctor. Dr. Dagen nodded. Renee smiled and got in the car. Her life was going to change today, she would see to that. Nothing was more important to her than her family now. She couldn't wait to get home.

Today was Thursday and Mike would be at a meeting, Andrew at practice and Nicole at the sitters. If she knew Devin, he would be playing his game. She couldn't wait to hug and kiss him. She could finally tell him that everything would be alright.

Devin was sitting in the recliner when she came in.

"What's wrong?" she asked after seeing the confused look on his face.

He sat there for a moment, silent. He lifted his head toward her and tilted it a little to the right, just noticing her, and said. "Nothing. Absolutely nothing."

Thank you for your purchase of the book. Please feel free to write a review at http://www.amazon.com/dp/B00FJGO8NU.

Born in Alton, IL / 1973

house she lived in
Junior High